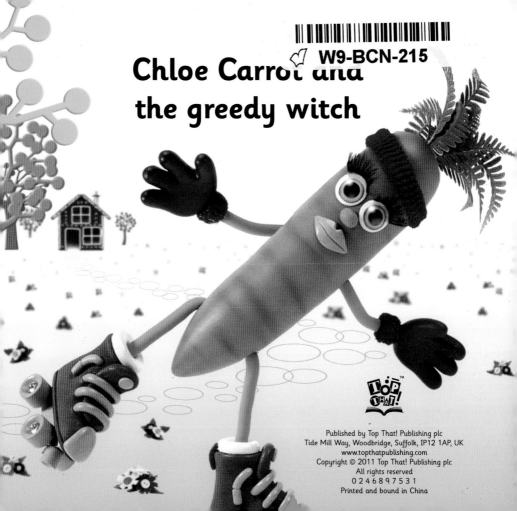

Chloe Carrot and the greedy witch

Published by Top That! Publishing plc
Tide Mill Way, Woodbridge, Suffolk, IP12 1AP, UK
www.topthatpublishing.com
Copyright © 2011 Top That! Publishing plc
All rights reserved
0 2 4 6 8 9 7 5 3 1
Printed and bound in China

What scene have the
children made today?

A magical woodland...

One day, Chloe Carrot stepped into the children's playscene. The children had created a magical woodland.

Looking around, Chloe spotted Little Jack Potato. He was about to eat a very large cake.

"Come for a walk, Little Jack," said Chloe. Reluctantly, Little Jack put down the cake and agreed.

After a long walk, Chloe and Little Jack were tired and hungry.
"Let's go home now, Chloe," said an exhausted Little Jack.

Then, Little Jack spotted something. It was a house made entirely of gingerbread, candy and frosting! It smelled and looked delicious! Little Jack was so hungry, that he ran over to taste it.

"Don't, Little Jack!" shouted Chloe. "That food isn't yours to take!"

But, Little Jack ignored Chloe's warning. He broke off a huge piece of gingerbread and stuffed it in his mouth!

"Mmm, delicious!" said Little Jack.

"HOW DARE YOU!" screeched a very angry-sounding voice...

Suddenly, the door flew open and a very angry witch appeared!

"How dare you eat my house!" screeched the witch. She quickly grabbed Little Jack, magicked up a cage and bundled him inside.

"If you want your friend to be released, you will obey every order I give you," the witch cackled to Chloe.

First, the witch demanded that Chloe fetch her water from the well on the other side of the woods.

As the angry witch waited for Chloe, she ate a huge piece of cake!

Behind the witch, Little Jack looked on, feeling very sad and very hungry.

When Chloe returned with the water the witch ordered her to make two pizzas.

"Won't a pizza make you feel ill after all that cake?" asked Chloe.

This made the witch very, very angry.

"If you want your friend back, you will do exactly as I say!" shouted the furious witch.

So, Chloe cooked two big pizzas. But, because Chloe is a very healthy Frooble, she made the witch a delicious salad too.

"**Y**uck!" said the witch, when Chloe brought over her meal. "What is this?"

"I made you a healthy salad," said Chloe. "It is good for you."

The witch tossed the salad away and Little Jack sadly watched as she ate every last crumb of each big pizza.

Talking with her mouth full of pizza, the witch made her next demand.

"Get me a bowl of ice cream!" shouted the witch, and Chloe did, even though the witch didn't say please.

The witch then ate the ice cream greedily and even licked the bowl!

As soon as she had finished her ice cream, the greedy witch began to complain again. She wanted more food!

"Fetch me two fruit pies with plenty of whipped cream!" screeched the witch.

Poor Chloe was very tired, but she fetched the pies. The greedy witch scoffed them in an instant!

Suddenly, the greedy witch began to feel very ill. Her tummy hurt and she felt very sick.

Now, most people would leave the greedy witch, but because Chloe is a very kind Frooble, she offered to look after her.

"**Q**uick! Get me out of here!" said Little Jack, when he saw that the witch was feeling sick.

"We can't leave her alone, Little Jack!" said Chloe. "She is not well."

"I'm very sorry that I didn't listen to you, Chloe," sighed Little Jack. "It is my fault we are in this mess!"

After a short sleep and some water the witch felt much better. "Thank you for looking after me," said the witch. "I know I was very mean, and far too greedy!"

"And I am sorry that I took your food without asking," said Little Jack.

The witch felt guilty for treating Chloe and Little Jack so badly and offered to make them a delicious breakfast.

"Only if it is healthy!" laughed Chloe.

The witch from the gingerbread house had learned her lesson and is no longer so greedy.

Now, Chloe loves to visit the witch. They even go roller-skating together!

And Little Jack will never take something that doesn't belong to him again!